Where's Emoji?

Where's
EMOJI?
SEEK AND FIND

Where's Emoji?

SIZZLE
P R E S S

THE EMOJIS ARE GOING ON VACATION!

MEET THE FAMILY!

THE EMOJIS ARE OFF ON THE TRIP OF A LIFETIME, TRAVELING AROUND THE WORLD AND SEEING THE SIGHTS. THE TROUBLE IS, THEY KEEP GETTING LOST! CAN YOU HELP THEM ON THEIR JOURNEY BY FINDING EVERY MEMBER OF THE EMOJI FAMILY IN EACH BUSY PICTURE?

SANDRA-EMOJI
THE MOM

SANDRA IS EXCITED TO TAKE THIS TRIP WITH HER FAMILY. SHE LOVES NATURE AND IS LOOKING FORWARD TO SEEING THE DIFFERENT FLOWERS OF THE WORLD.

BOB-EMOJI
THE DAD

BOB WANTS HIS CHILDREN TO SEE THE MANY WONDERS OF THE WORLD ON THIS VACATION. HE LOVES HISTORY AND WANTS TO LEARN MORE ABOUT ANCIENT CIVILIZATIONS.

EXTRA HIDDEN CHARACTERS

THERE ARE SIX EXTRA EMOJIS HIDDEN ON EACH PAGE. CAN YOU SPOT THEM ALL?

EDDIE
THE TOURIST
EDDIE LOVES TRAVELING, AND IS EAGER TO VISIT AS MANY COUNTRIES AS POSSIBLE.

MO
THE PHOTOGRAPHE
MO IS BUILDING HIS PORTFOLIO BY SNAPPING PHOTOS ON EVERY CONTINE

LONZO-EMOJI
THE TWEEN

LONZO IS THE MOST EXCITABLE FAMILY MEMBER. HE LOVES TO EAT TASTY FOOD AND HE'S LOOKING FORWARD TO TRYING DIFFERENT CUISINES.

ELLA-EMOJI
THE TEEN

ELLA IS ONE STYLISH AND SPORTY EMOJI. SHE'S LOOKING FORWARD TO SHOPPING AROUND THE WORLD, SHE ALSO CAN'T WAIT TO GO SURFING IN HAWAII.

KIKI-EMOJI
THE BABY

KIKI LOVES COLORS AND WANTS TO COLLECT ANYTHING THAT'S BRIGHT OR SHINY. THE FAMILY WILL NEED TO KEEP AN EYE ON THIS PLAYFUL BABY!

REX-EMOJI
FAMILY PET

REX HAS A SECRET WISH THE FAMILY DOESN'T KNOW ABOUT. THIS BOUNCY BUNNY IS LOOKING FORWARD TO MEETING OTHER CUTE CRITTERS.

ROBYN
THE TOUR GUIDE
ROBYN IS GUIDING THE OJIS AROUND THE WORLD, IS ALWAYS GETTING LOST!

JACK
THE BUSINESSMAN
JACK MISSES OUT ON ALL THE SIGHTS BECAUSE HE'S ALWAYS TAKING AN IMPORTANT CALL.

ALVIN
THE ESCAPEE
ALVIN HAS ESCAPED FROM THE ZOO SO THAT HE CAN SEE THE WORLD.

LISS
THE FRIEND
LISS IS TRAVELING WITH EDDIE AND BECOMES GOOD FRIENDS WITH ELLA.

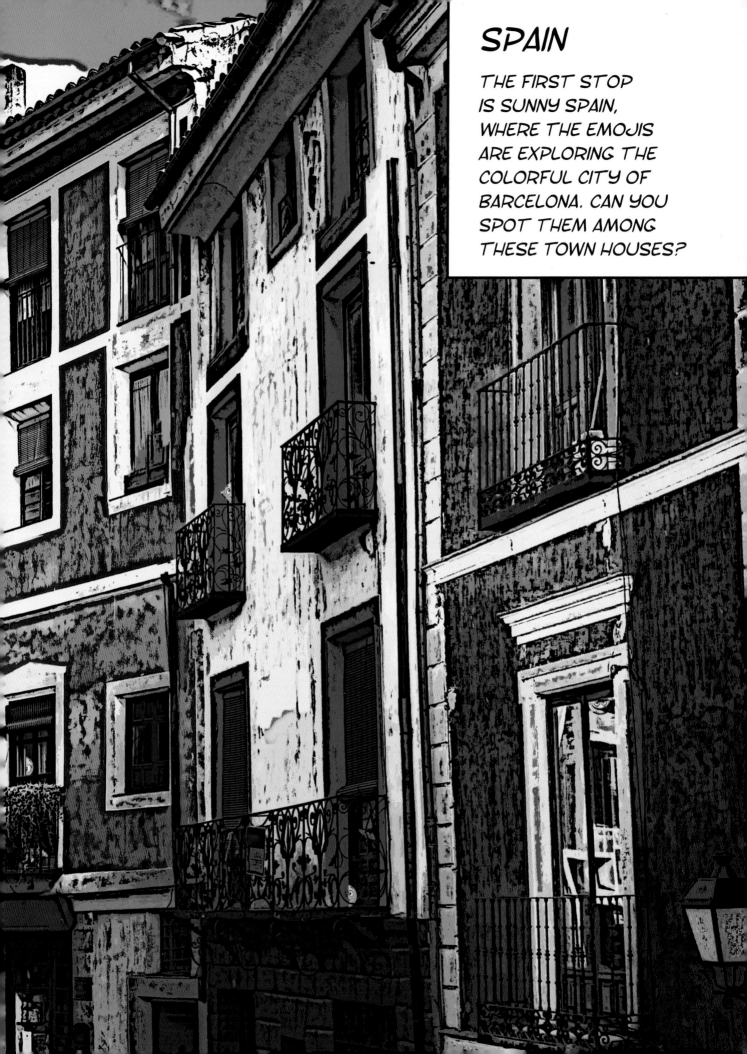

SPAIN

THE FIRST STOP IS SUNNY SPAIN, WHERE THE EMOJIS ARE EXPLORING THE COLORFUL CITY OF BARCELONA. CAN YOU SPOT THEM AMONG THESE TOWN HOUSES?

HOLLAND

SANDRA-EMOJI LOVES FLOWERS AND WANTS TO SEE THE TULIP FIELDS IN HOLLAND, BUT HER FAMILY IS NOW LOST AMONG THE THOUSANDS OF FLOWERS! CAN YOU FIND ALL THE EMOJIS?

ITALY

LONZO-EMOJI LOVES PIZZA, SO THE EMOJIS STOP OFF ON THE ITALIAN COAST. THE FAMILY SPLITS UP TO SEARCH FOR THE PERFECT PIZZERIA. CAN YOU FIND ALL THE FAMILY MEMBERS?

THE U.S.A.

AFTER A LONG FLIGHT, THE EMOJIS ARRIVE IN NEW YORK CITY. THERE'S SO MUCH TO SEE, AND LOTS OF PLACES IN WHICH TO GET LOST! CAN YOU SPOT THE FAMILY IN TIMES SQUARE?

MEXICO

THE EMOJIS ARRIVE IN MEXICO DURING THE DAY OF THE DEAD CELEBRATIONS. IT'S SO BUSY THERE THAT THEY SOON GET LOST. CAN YOU FIND THEM ALL IN THIS COLORFUL ART DISPLAY?

HAWAII

ELLA-EMOJI WANTS TO LEARN HOW TO SURF, BUT WILL SHE BE ABLE TO STAY ON THE BOARD? THE FAMILY HEADS TO THE BEACH FOR A DAY OF FUN. CAN YOU SPOT EACH EMOJI?

CHILE

THE EMOJIS LOVE SEEING THE BRIGHTLY-COLORED FABRICS IN THIS CHILEAN MARKET. SANDRA-EMOJI CHOOSES A NEW HAT AND ELLA-EMOJI IS INSPIRED BY THE BEAUTIFUL PATTERNS. CAN YOU FIND EACH OF THE EMOJIS?

BRAZIL

IT'S CARNIVAL TIME IN RIO DE JANEIRO. THE EMOJIS JOIN IN THE PARADE BUT CAN'T FIND EACH OTHER ONCE THE CELEBRATION IS OVER. CAN YOU FIND ALL THE FAMILY MEMBERS?

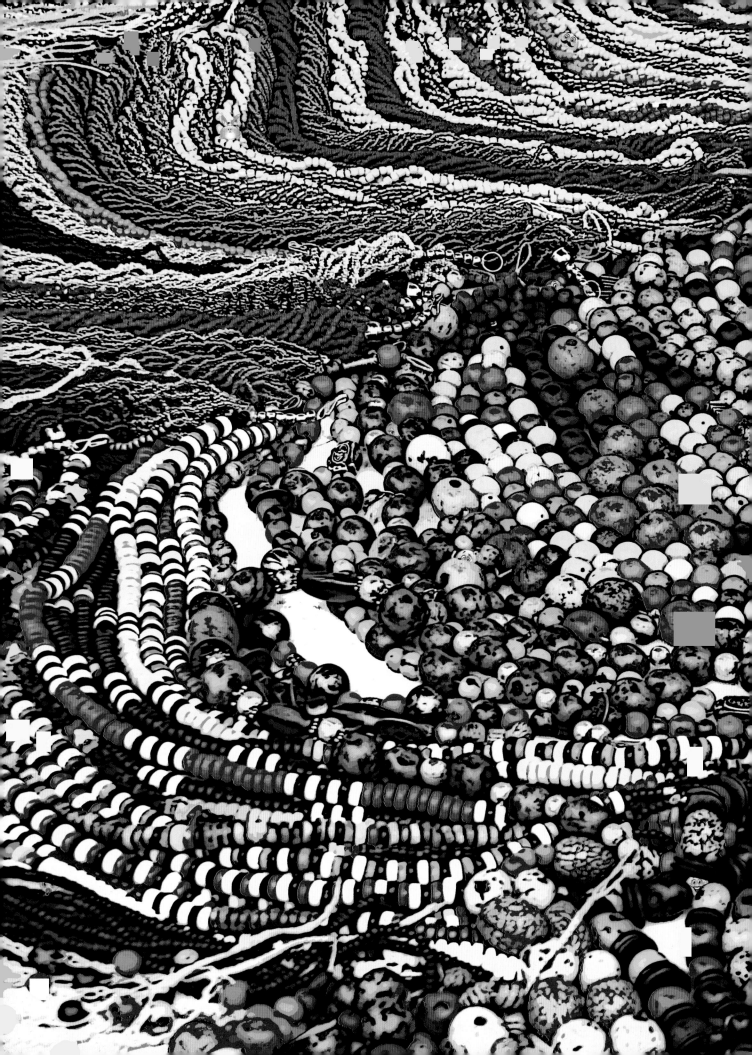

EQUADOR

KIKI-EMOJI LOVES THE PRETTY, COLORFUL BEADS THAT ARE SOLD IN THIS WARM SOUTH AMERICAN COUNTRY. SHE DIVES RIGHT IN TO CHECK THEM OUT. THE FAMILY SPLITS UP TO FIND HER! CAN YOU FIND THEM ALL?

NAMIBIA

ON A SAFARI TRIP IN AFRICA, THE EMOJIS SPOT THIS FRIENDLY ANTELOPE AND TRY TO GET CLOSER. CAN YOU SPOT THE WHOLE FAMILY BEFORE THE ANTELOPE RUNS AWAY?

MOROCCO

THE FAMILY SPLITS UP TO FIND THE PERFECT GIFT FOR GRANDMA-EMOJI IN THE COLORFUL BAZAARS OF MOROCCO. CAN YOU FIND ALL THE EMOJIS AMONG THE SLIPPERS?

EGYPT

BOB-EMOJI HAS ALWAYS WANTED TO SEE THE EGYPTIAN PYRAMIDS. DURING THE BUMPY CAMEL RIDE TO GIZA, THE FAMILY GETS SPLIT UP! CAN YOU FIND THEM ALL?

JAPAN

TOKYO IS A BUSY CITY, NO MATTER WHAT TIME OF DAY IT IS! THE FAMILY SOON GETS LOST IN THE HUSTLE AND BUSTLE. CAN YOU FIND THEM ALL SO THEY CAN CONTINUE THEIR JOURNEY?

INDIA

THE MARKETS OF INDIA ARE FULL OF EXOTIC SPICES AND FRUITS. THE EMOJIS WANT TO TRY EVERYTHING! CAN YOU FIND THE WHOLE FAMILY AT THIS MARKET STALL?

CHINA

THE SKYSCRAPERS IN CHINA ARE AN AMAZING SIGHT. THE EMOJI FAMILY STARTS EXPLORING, BUT SOON GETS LOST! CAN YOU HELP FIND THEM ALL?

THE GREAT BARRIER REEF

THERE ARE SO MANY BEAUTIFUL THINGS TO SEE UNDER THE SEA! CAN YOU SPOT ALL THE EMOJIS AMONG THE COLORFUL CORAL?

NEW ZEALAND

FROM SNOWCAPPED MOUNTAINS TO FIELDS FULL OF FLOWERS, THERE IS SO MUCH TO SEE ON THE ISLANDS OF NEW ZEALAND. CAN YOU FIND WHERE EACH OF THE EMOJIS ARE?

AUSTRALIA

THE EMOJIS TAKE SOME TIME OUT FROM THEIR BUSY VACATION TO RELAX ON THE SANDY BEACHES OF AUSTRALIA. CAN YOU FIND THEM ALL BEFORE THEIR NEXT FLIGHT?

ANTARCTICA

REX-EMOJI HAS A SECRET WISH—TO BE A PENGUIN! HE HOPS OFF AND HIDES IN THIS PENGUIN COLONY. THE FAMILY GETS LOST TRYING TO FIND HIM. CAN YOU FIND THEM ALL?

Where's EMOJI?

ANSWERS

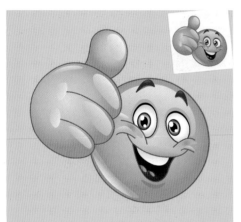

DID YOU
SPOT THE
BLUE-EMOJI?

DID YOU
T THE
EMOJI?

DID YOU SPOT THE SCIENTIST-EMOJI?

DID YOU SPOT THE SUPER-EMOJI?

DID YOU SPOT THE ARMY-EMOJI?

DID YOU
SPOT THE
SURFER-EMOJI?

DID YOU
SPOT THE
SLEEPY-EMOJI?

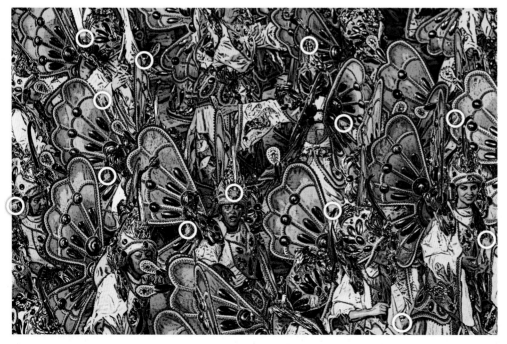

DID YOU
SPOT THE
GUITAR-EMOJI?

DID YOU SPOT THE SCO-EMOJI?

DID YOU SPOT THE EARTH-EMOJI?

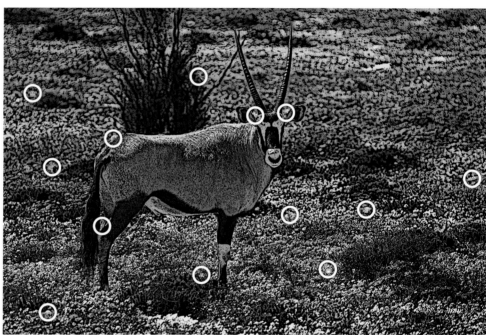

DID YOU SPOT THE -EMOJI?

DID YOU
SPOT THE
MUMMY-EMOJI?

DID YOU
SPOT THE
ASTRO-EMOJI?

DID YOU
SPOT THE
HUNGRY-EMOJI?

DID YOU
SPOT THE
BUSINESS-EMOJI?

DID YOU
SPOT THE
RAIN-EMOJI?

DID YOU
SPOT THE
SPOOKY-EMOJI?

DID YOU SPOT THE ...-EMOJI?

DID YOU SPOT THE ...OR-EMOJI?